In-o-saur, Out-o-saur

David Bedford and Leonie Worthington

Up-o-saur

Down-o-saur

In-o-saur

Out-o-saur

Slow-o-saur

FAST-o-saur

Roar-o-saur

Long-o-saur

Short-o-saur

Front-o-saur

Back-o-saur

Over-o-saur

Under-o-saur

Awake-o-saur

ASLeep-o-saur

Open-o-saur

Closed-o-saur

Big-o-saur

Small-o-saur

Hot-o-saur

Cold-o-saur

Little Hare Books
4/21 Mary Street, Surry Hills
NSW 2010 AUSTRALIA

www.littleharebooks.com

National Library of Australia
Cataloguing-in-Publication entry

Bedford, David, 1969-.
In-o-saur, out-o-saur.

For pre-school children.
ISBN 1 877003 85 9.

1. Polarity – Juvenile literature. 2. English language –
Synonyms and antonyms – Juvenile literature. 3. Dinosaurs –
Juvenile literature. I. Worthington, Leonie, 1956-. II. Title.

428.1

Designed by Serious Business
Produced by Phoenix Offset, Hong Kong
Printed in China

5 4 3 2 1